Ask Me

by Bernard Waber

illustrated by Suzy Lee

Houghton Mifflin Harcourt
Boston • New York

Ask me what I like.

What do you like?

I like dogs.
I like cats.
I like turtles.

I like geese.

Geese in the sky? Or geese in the water?

I like geese in the sky.
No, in the water. I like both.

Ask me what else I like.

What else do you like?

I like frogs.
I like frogs swimming.
And frogs hopping.

I like bugs.

Insects?

No, bugs.

I like butterflies.
And lightning bugs.

Fireflies?

No, lightning bugs.

And I like beetles, and bumblebees, and dragonflies.
And I like flowers.
   No, I love flowers. Bees love flowers too. Right?

   Right.

And bees make honey. Right?

Right.

Ask me what else I like.

What else do you like?

I like horses. No, I like riding horses.

You rode a horse?

On the merry-go-round. Remember?
You remember.

I remember.

Ask me if I like ice cream cones.

Do you like ice cream cones?

No. I love, love, love ice cream cones.

What else do I like?

What else do you like?

I like sand. I like digging in the sand. I really, really do like
digging in the sand. Deep, deep, down, down in the sand.

And I like seashells.
Remember when we collected seashells?

I remember.

And I like starfish.

Ask me some more *I likes*.

How about some more *I likes*?

I like the color red. I like red everything.

Ask me what else.

What else?

I like rain. I like splishing, sploshing,
and splooshing in the rain.

Splishing, sploshing, and *splooshing.*
I like those words.

They're rain words. I made them up.

I know.

Ask me what else I like.

What else do you like?

I like stories.
I like stories about bears.

Now ask me a *How come*?

All right, how about a *How come*?

How come birds build nests?

All right. How come birds build nests?

You tell it.

Ask me another *I like*.

All right. How about another *I like*?

I'm thinking.

I'm waiting.

I know.

What?

So they will have a safe place to lay their eggs.

I knew that.

Why did you ask?

Because I like to hear you tell it.

Next Thursday.

What about next Thursday?

I like next Thursday.
    Do you know why I like next Thursday?

Why do you like next Thursday?

Because next Thursday is what?

What?

My birthday. You knew that.

How could I ever forget?

You wouldn't.

Wouldn't what?

Forget my birthday.

Not in a million years would I forget your birthday.

How about a billion years?

Not even in a billion years.

That's better.

And you won't forget that I like balloons, party hats, games, and a big cake that says *Happy Birthday*?

I won't forget.

Now ask me if I am sleepy.

Are you sleepy?

No, I am not sleepy. Well, a little sleepy.
No, I am a whole lot sleepy.

How about if we say good night?

Where's my teddy?

Here's your teddy.

And my kangaroo?

Here's your kangaroo.

Good night.

Good night.
Please leave the door open.

The door is open.

Good night.

Wait. Ask me something else.

What?

Ask me if I want another good night kiss.

Would you like another good night kiss?

Yes, I would like another good night kiss.

Good night.

Good night.